D0606663

For Graham and Cole —M. R.

For Sylvia, with great admiration —E. C.

Farrar Straus Giroux Books for Young Readers
An imprint of Macmillan Publishing Group, LLC
120 Broadway, New York, NY 10271

Text copyright © 2021 by Maggie C. Rudd
Pictures copyright © 2021 by Elisa Chavarri
All rights reserved
Color separations by Embassy Graphics
Printed in China by RR Donnelley Asia Printing Solutions Ltd., Dongguan City,
Guangdong Province
Designed by Aram Kim
First edition, 2021
10 9 8 7 6 5 4 3 2 1
mackids.com
Library of Congress Cataloging-in-Publication Data is available.
ISBN 978-0-374-31413-2
Our books may be purchased in bulk for promotional, educational, or
business use. Please contact your local bookseller or the Macmillan
Corporate and Premium Sales Department at (800) 221-7945 ext. 5442 or
by email at MacmillanSpecialMarkets@macmillan.com.

Rudd, Maggie,
I'll hold your hand /
2021.
33305250899444
ca   03/25/22

I'LL HOLD YOUR HAND

Maggie C. Rudd

Illustrated by
Elisa Chavarri

Farrar Straus Giroux
New York

I'll hold your hand

on the night you arrive

when the whole world comes alive.

When you're learning to crawl

and you stumble and fall,
I'll hold your hand.

when new things are scary
or monsters too hairy.

When thunder is clashing
and lightning is flashing,

I'll hold your hand.

I'll hold your hand

when you walk, then you run,
and the fun's just begun!

When waves are crashing

or puddles need splashing,

I'll hold your hand.

I'll hold your hand

when we look both ways

or our bus gets delayed.

On the first day of school
or when words can be cruel,

I'll hold your hand.

I'll hold your hand

when good news is calling

SCHOOL CANCELLATIONS

or the first snow is falling.

On your first night away

if you decide not to stay,

I'll hold your hand.

I'll hold your hand

when the going gets tough
and hugs aren't enough.

If love ever hurts you

or words desert you,

I'll hold your hand.

I'll hold your hand

when the days end too soon

and we wait for the moon.

When you're counting sheep
and you're falling asleep,
I'll hold your hand.

I'll hold your hand

in the winter

or summer

when goodbyes are a bummer.

In the spring or the fall,

when you're feeling small,

or for no reason at all,

I'll hold your hand.